THE SURPRISE SLEEPOVER

Created by Kenn Viselman

Written by Scott Stabile and Catherine Lyon

Published by Jay At Play Publishing

Copyright © 2005 KVIP, Inc.
Licensed by Kenn Viselman presents . . . All rights reserved. Printed in China.
No part of this book may be reproduced in any manner whatsoever without the written permission of KVp. For information address Jay At Play Publishing, 295 Fifth Avenue, New York, NY 10016.

For information please write:
Special Markets Department, Jay At Play Publishing, 295 Fifth Avenue, New York, NY 10016.

ISBN 0-9772256-3-1

Jay At Play Publishing is a trademark of Jay Franco & Sons, Inc.

First printing: October 2005

Visit Li'l Pet Hospital on the World Wide Web at
www.lilpethospital.com

10 9 8 7 6 5 4 3 2 1

Dear Parents:

The most wonderful thing in children's lives is the love they receive from their families. Children derive tremendous pleasure from imitating their parents' care in pretend play and make-believe.

The Li'l Pets in Healy Fields are much like young children in their high spirits, rambunctiousness, and curiosity, as well as in their need to be loved and nurtured. They spend their days playing games, sharing stories, and exploring the world around them. When the adventures are just too much for the Li'l Pets to handle by themselves, the delightful Dr. Foxx is always there to fix their boo-boos and make them feel well and happy again. Then all they need is a li'l extra love from you.

Welcome to the loving and lovable world of the Li'l Pet Hospital!

With all good wishes,

Kenn Viselman

Kenn Viselman

The small cut on Limit the Puppy's back paw was sore and red. Limit sat very still as Dr. Foxx gently examined it. He was very brave.

Dr. Foxx said to him,
"Well, now, Limit, to treat this right
You must stay here for just one night.
I know that it may frighten you
To sleep someplace that's strange and new."

"Frighten me?" Limit barked loudly.
"I am not afraid of anything! I'll stay
in the hospital! I'll stay a week! I'll
stay a month! I'll stay--"

"Hold on. We won't need that much time.
In just one day you should be fine,"
said Dr. Foxx with a smile.

Dr. Foxx led Limit upstairs to a cozy
room with a big window and a large,
soft bed.

"It's not your own, but nonetheless,
It ought to do for one night's rest"

Limit slowly climbed into the bed, and crept under the blanket. It was a red blanket. Limit's blanket at home was blue and fuzzy and always smelled like fresh green grass.

"Now rest that paw and it will mend.
You'll soon be back with all your friends."

Dr. Foxx patted Limit on the head as
he walked toward the door.

Limit tucked his nose under the strange red blanket. He sniffed around for his favorite chew toy, but his favorite chew toy was at home.

Suddenly, there was a knock at the door. It was Dropsie the Bear Cub. "Hi, Limit!" Dropsie said. He tossed something to Limit. "Here! Catch!"

It was Limit's favorite blue blanket! "I know you don't like to sleep without your blue blanket."

"Thank you, Dropsie!" said Limit as he pulled the blue blanket closely around him.

Knock, Knock. Someone else was at the door.

"Come in!" called Limit.

Splint the Bunny and Loveblossom the Pony came in. "Hi, Limit!" they said. Loveblossom pulled something out of her bag. "May I put this up on the wall?" she asked.

It was a beautiful picture of all of Limit's L'il Pet Hospital friends.

"We know how much you like this picture," said Loveblossom. "When we heard you were in the hospital, we went to your house and got it." Loveblossom held up the picture and Splint carefully put tape on each of the corners. "Now your room will feel a little more like home."

"Thank you, Loveblossom!" said
Limit. "And thank you, Splint!" He
turned to see the wonderful picture
that his good friends had brought
him

Just then, another knock came at the door. "Come in!" Limit called.

The door opened, and in walked Scuffs the Kitten, with her tail held high in the air. She pranced over to the bed and dropped something on it. It was Limit's best chew toy!

"How can a puppy sleep anywhere without
a chew toy?" Scuffs asked. "That's the
first thought I had when I heard you
needed to stay here."
She sat down beside Limit's bed, and
began to wash.

"Thank you, Scuffs!" said Limit as he took
the chew toy gently in his mouth.

A little later Dr. Foxx came into Limit's room with a supper tray. It held a bowl of oatmeal and a dish of milk. He put the tray down on a table near Limit.

"The stars and moon are in the sky.
And you must tell your friends good-bye.
Suppertime is here tonight,
And soon we must put out the lights."

"Suppertime, Limit! Have to go now," said Dropsie. Splint and Loveblossom waved goodbye. Scuffs blew him a kiss. "Get well soon!" they called.

The room was suddenly still. Limit looked at the large bowl of oatmeal in front of him. He thought of all the good things he had to eat at home. Slowly he picked up the spoon. He was about to take a bite when he heard a sound.

He sat up straight. He listened. He
sniffed. Something was coming
down the hall. Something that
smelled delicious. Something tastier
than oatmeal.

There was a quick knock at the door and in came Filo the Lion Cub with the largest picnic basket that Limit had ever seen!

"Suppertime" cried Filo. "A simply delicious supper for Limit!" He pulled out a large red-checked tablecloth and laid it on Limit's bed. "What'll you have, my friend?"

"Oh," said Limit. "I'd like scrambled eggs, Filo. And hot dogs. And a hamburger! And lots and lots of ice cream! And French fries! With ketchup!"

Filo looked in the basket. "Eggs, hot dogs, hamburgers, French fries, ketchup, and ice cream! It's all here!"

Limit ate and ate and ate. He was so full that when he finished his last scoop of ice cream, he put down the spoon and closed his eyes.

Very quickly, Filo picked up Limit's dishes and gently took the spoon from his paw. He wiped them clean with a paper towel and put everything back in his picnic basket.

Then Filo took out a small harmonica
and played a soft, sweet, lullabye.

Limit's head dropped to the pillow.
His favorite blue blanket was
wrapped snugly around him and his
nose on his favorite chew toy.

Filo finished his song. Then he went to the door of Limit's room and turned off the lights.

"Filo?" called Limit sleepily. "Are you still here?"

"Of course," said Filo. "Of course I'm here. I'm going to stay right beside you. Now you just rest and get well."

"Thank you, Filo," said Limit.

"You're welcome," said Filo.

Dr. Foxx came by Limit's room to
check on him a little while later. Limit
was sound asleep in his bed. Filo was
curled up in the chair beside him.

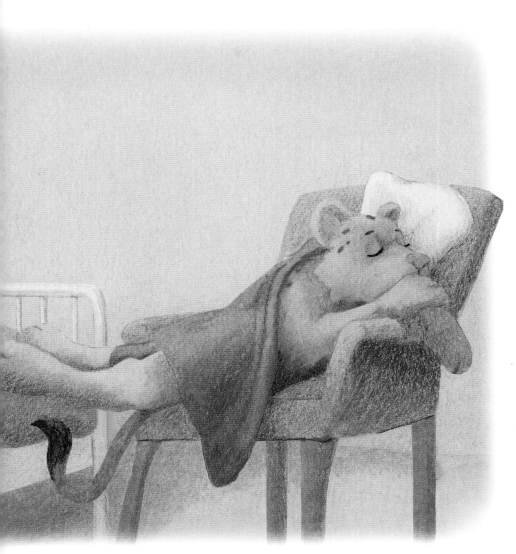

Dr. Foxx gently covered Filo with
the red blanket.

"Good night. Sleep tight," Dr.Foxx
whispered as he tiptoed out of the room.

And now... All they need is

a li'l extra love from you!

Dr. Foxx says:

If you scrape your leg or arm,
Clean the cut, there'll be no harm.

There's no need to feel too blue,
Soon you will be as good as new.

Now give your pet a great big hug,
And tuck him in so he'll feel sung.